Thisbook belongs to

_____

Mister
Tom T. Hall

CHRISTMAS
and
THE OLD HOUSE

Illustrated by
Laura L. Seeley

PEACHTREE PUBLISHERS, LTD.
ATLANTA ○ MEMPHIS

Published by
Peachtree Publishers, Ltd.
494 Armour Circle, NE
Atlanta, Georgia 30324

Manufactured in the United States of America

10 9 8 7 6 5 4 3 2 1

Cover illustrations by Laura L. Seeley

Library of Congress Cataloging-in-Publication Data

Hall, Tom T.
    Christmas and the old house.

    Summary: Bobby and Brenda learn a lesson about forgiveness and
the Christmas spirit when they sneak into an abandoned house and
decorate a tree they find growing through the floor.
    [1. Christmas trees—Fiction. 2. Dwellings—Fiction. 3. Christmas—
Fiction] I. Seeley, Laura L., 1958-   ill.   II. Title.
PZ7.H1488 1989 [Fic]   89-15942
ISBN 0-934601-91-7

It was a week before Christmas and the sun was shining. Brenda and I live where the sun shines a lot.

Brenda is seven and I am almost six. We are so old we don't have to show our fingers anymore. We know some things about the numbers six and seven. Our mothers and fathers are big people. My father can see on top of the refrigerator.

Brenda's house is next to mine.

Brenda's house is next to mine. We don't live on a street. On a street there are places to walk on the side. We live on a road. On a road there is only a fence on the side. Over the fence on our road there are cows. And sometimes a bull will chase you. On a street there are places to shop and buy things. We live on a road.

Brenda is seven and I am almost six and so she is older. She is also braver and maybe smarter. She went to school last year. And I don't get to go until next year when I am six. When you get old, you get brave.

Brenda said, "Let's go to The Old House."

I said, "We can't go to The Old House." I always say, "We can't go to The Old House." Brenda said, "Bobby. You're a 'fraidy cat." That's my name—Bobby.

I said, "I'm not old enough to be brave."

To get to The Old House we had to cross the hard road in front of our houses and go up a grassy road and then walk through the trees. From The Old House you have to look hard to see our houses.

The people who used to live there moved away from The Old House. Our parents told us that they took everything.

There's nothing in it. No television and no chairs and no lights. Nothing. It will scare us to death. Or that's what our parents say.

That's why Brenda wanted to go there. She says it's fun to be afraid when there's nothing to be afraid of.

So we went to The Old House and looked at the broken windows and the fallen-down doors. Brenda wanted to get close and look inside. She wanted to see if it was really empty the way our parents said.

We stood and looked at The Old House for a minute. Then Brenda, who's afraid of nothing to be afraid of, turned and started running away. When we got back out on The Grassy Road, we laughed.

If I do something wrong or something upsets me, my mother makes me tell her.

Here's what happened: She said, "Did you and Brenda go to The Old House?" I pretended I was learning to tie my shoe. I said, "What?"

She said, "You heard me." She always says, "You heard me."

She said, "Did you and Brenda go to The Old House?" I was still learning to tie my shoe. I said, "What?"

She said, "When your father gets home, he'll talk to

We went back to The Old House the next day.

you, young man."

I said, "Everybody makes mistakes." I had heard my mother say that.

When my father got home, he spanked me for not answering my mother. Everybody can make mistakes except me.

Brenda's father never spanks her. Her father talks and talks and talks. Brenda said she would rather be spanked than hear the talk, talk, talk. I would rather talk.

We went back to The Old House the next day. There is grass on the road where we walk to get there. That's why we call it The Grassy Road. Brenda went first. My mother told me to play with Brenda. When she went to The Old House, I had to go. I was playing with her. When I play with Brenda, I go where she goes because she is older and braver. We walked slower when we got near. Even Brenda said there might be something to be afraid of.

Brenda yelled, "Anybody in there?" My heart went fast. Brenda yelled again. "Anybody home?"

I yelled, "Come on out!"

When I yell, Brenda always says, "Shhhh!"

We went a little closer. I was behind Brenda. She said, "Look. Wow! A Christmas tree!"

I said, "A what?" I looked into the house, and there it was, a little green tree like a Christmas tree growing out of the floor of The Old House. It was as tall as Brenda. We stood and looked at the tree.

Brenda said, "It's growing out of the floor."

I said, "I see it."

Brenda said, "Let's go make some plans."

We ran to The Planning Rock. That's where we go to talk. It is a big rock that we have to climb up on. Brenda went first and then pulled me up by the hand. We sat on The Planning Rock and talked about the tree. Brenda said, "We need to plan on what to do with the tree."

I thought hard. I couldn't think of anything. It was just a tree. Brenda said, "It's a Christmas tree. What do people do with Christmas trees?"

I said, "They use them for Christmas." I was happy I said that.

Brenda said, "We'll decorate it."

I said, "How?"

She said, "Can you get some ribbon?"

I said, "Why can't you get some?"

Brenda knew my mother had some ribbon. That's why she asked.

She said, "Folly-o-do!" She always says, "Folly-o-do." It doesn't mean anything, and that's why she says it so much.

I said, "I can maybe get some."

She said, "I'll get some popcorn and some pop tabs."

Brenda saves the tabs from the cans of soda pop that we get sometimes.

I said, "Why are we going to decorate the tree?"

Brenda said, "Because."

I said, "I don't like becauses."

She said, "Because it's Christmas. We'll decorate it for Jesus and not tell anyone."

Christmas is Jesus' birthday. Even I knew that.

I said, "And we'll get Jesus a present."

Brenda said, "We can't get a present."

I said, "Why?"

She said, "We don't have any money."

I said, "I'm not old enough to worry about money. My mother said that."

Brenda said, "Folly-o-do."

We sat there talking for a long, exciting time about decorating the Christmas tree in The Old House just for Jesus. Brenda was so full of plans it made me crazy. She talked and talked about it. I said, "Who else will see it?"

She said, "What?"

It sounded like me talking to my mother. I said, "Who else will see the tree if we decorate it?"

Brenda said, "Only Jesus, of course."

I said, "And Santa Claus."

Brenda looked at me with a mean look. "No," she said. "This is not a Santa Claus tree."

Brenda was so full of plans it made me crazy.

I said, "Why?"

She said, "Well. Because."

I started to say I did not like becauses, but Brenda already knew that.

I said, "What if we get caught going to The Old House? It won't be a surprise anymore."

Brenda bounced her shoulders up and down. She always bounces her shoulders up and down. She said, "That's why we have to plan. So we won't get caught and ruin Jesus' surprise."

I said, "We got a tree for Jesus already—one at your house and one at mine."

She said, "No, no. Those trees are for us. Do you put presents for Jesus under your tree?"

I said, "No."

She said, "See! We take Jesus' presents to church and give them to the preacher and he gives them to Jesus. Right?"

I didn't want to, but I said, "Right."

Brenda said, "But that way Jesus never gets a tree of his own. Right?"

I said, "Right."

We sat on The Planning Rock and talked some more. I don't think Brenda knew Jesus as well as I did. Because she thinks you can do something scary and not tell anybody and still surprise Jesus. And I don't think so. But we did it anyway. Because it was fun. I guess.

I got the ribbon from a drawer where my mother keeps the scissors. I am not allowed to run with the scissors in my hand.   I might fall and stick myself.   I

didn't run with the scissors. I
cut some ribbon off of the roll
and put it inside my shirt. I
closed the drawer and started back
to The Grassy Road. My mother was
standing by the fence talking to
Brenda's mother.

She called to me, "Bobby, where are you going?"
I said, "To play with Brenda."
She said, "What are you doing?"
I said, "Nothing."
She said, "What were you doing in the house?"
I said, "I came to get my coat."
She said, "Couldn't you find it?"
I said, "I'm not cold."
She said, "It's chilly. Go put it on."

I said, "Yes, ma'am."

I went back in the house to get my coat, but I could still hear my mother saying something to Brenda's mother. I couldn't hear what it was she said, but she usually says something like, "He would lose his head if it weren't tied on." Something like that.

I ran back to The Planning Rock to meet Brenda. I was breathing hard when I got there and climbed up on the rock where Brenda was already sitting.

She said, "Did you get the ribbon?"
I said, "Yes, and I almost got caught."
She said, "Did you get caught?"
I said, "No. Almost."
She said, "Exciting, isn't it?"

I said, "No." Brenda thinks it's fun to be afraid when there's nothing to be afraid of.

I said, "What did you get?"
She held out a handful
of those tabs that come off
the soda and shine. "I've been
saving them for something
special like this." Brenda saves
a lot of neat stuff like that.

We went back to The Old House and decorated the tree. The old boards had rotted and turned into dirt where the tree was growing. There was a big hole in the roof where the sun was shining in. We tied the ribbons all over the limbs. Brenda tied the shiny pop tabs in places where there weren't any ribbons. The door of The

Old House had fallen off its hinges. A breeze came through the door and went out the window. The ribbons waved and the tabs turned every which way, and the sunshine through the roof made the tabs and the ribbons shine. It looked like a real Christmas tree. Brenda jumped up and down and laughed. I did, too. It was the best thing we'd ever done. Brenda said, "Now, let's get back to The Planning Rock and make some plans."

We sat on The Planning Rock for a long time. We looked toward The Old House and felt good. It was exciting to know that our decorated tree was there and nobody else in the whole world knew about it. Brenda finally said, "We'll leave a note that says, *We love you, Jesus*."

I said, "And we'll put our names on there."
Brenda said, "Yes."

It looked like a real Christmas tree.

We didn't say anything for a little bit. Then I said, "I can't write."

Brenda said, "Don't worry. I can write it. Can you write your name?"

I said, "I can write Bobby."

She said, "Well, that's your name, isn't it?"

I said, "My important name is Robert. But I can write Bobby because my mother showed me how to do it."

Brenda said, "If your mother knows you're Bobby, then Jesus does, too."

I said, "I guess so. Jesus knows everything anyway."

And so Brenda said, "I'll write the note and bring it to The Planning Rock tomorrow. And we'll both write our names on it and put it under the tree."

That night at my house I had to go get ready for bed.

I was in my room and I could hear my parents in the kitchen. They were talking.

I sat on my bed and wondered what they were talking about. I hoped they weren't talking about The Old House. It made my stomach hurt when I thought they might have found Jesus' surprise tree in The Old House. I wasn't in my room for very long.

My mother came in and sat down on my bed beside me. She ran her fingers through my hair the way she does sometimes. She said, "Bobby, how would you like a piece of pie before bedtime?"

So we went into the kitchen and I could tell that the house smelled different. Not really funny exactly, but kind of yummy. Our house smells the same except for party times. I thought this must be the Christmas smell.

I had a piece of apple pie with ice cream on top before I went to bed. That night I had a bad dream. In the dream my father and mother were standing looking at the Christmas tree in The Old House, and they both looked sad because no one had told them about Jesus' tree.

The next day was a cold day. I had to wear my extra warm coat and a pair of mittens before I could go play with Brenda. I hate mittens. When Brenda knocked on the door and asked for me, she was wearing a pair of gloves. I asked my mother if I could wear gloves. She said, "Maybe you will get some gloves for Christmas. Now go and play."

On the way up The Grassy Road Brenda said, "I guess you will get a pair of gloves for Christmas."

"No," I said. "I want a truck."

She said, "I think you will get a pair of gloves."

Brenda is smart like that.

We went to The Planning Rock. The wind was blowing cold. Brenda took a piece of paper from her pocket and unfolded it. She laid it on the rock and said, "See there? It says, *We love you, Jesus.*" She said, "There's my name right there. You put yours right here." She pointed to a place on the note. I put my name on the paper and held it out to look at it. It was beautiful.

Brenda said, "Come on." She jumped off The Planning Rock. We walked toward The Old House.

When we got close to the house, Brenda hollered, "Anybody home?"

A great big voice said, "YES, MAY I HELP YOU?"

Brenda knocked me down turning around to run. I jumped up and started after her as fast as I could go. We fell down three times before we got to The Planning Rock. As we were running, we could hear the big voice saying, "HELLO? HELLO?"

We sat down behind The Planning Rock and breathed hard for a long time. Brenda said, "You think he saw us?"

I said, "Who was it?"

Brenda breathed some more. She said, "A man. A big man with a hat. I saw him."

Brenda knocked me down turning around to run.

I said, "Oh. I thought it was Jesus."

Brenda said, "No, it was a big man with a hat. He was kneeling down by the tree. He stood up when I hollered."
"Did he see us?"
"Maybe, maybe not."
I said, "I'm going home!"
Brenda said, "Where's the note?"
I said, "You had it."
I said, "It's got our names on it. If he finds the note, he'll know who we are."
Brenda said, "You're right. Let's sneak back and look . . . see what he's doing."
I said, "I want to go home."
Brenda said, "No, you can't go home now. You're in this, too. We got to take a look. Come on, we'll sneak behind the trees."

Brenda started walking low to the ground. I followed her even lower to the ground. We went from tree to tree until we could see The Old House. There was a bush between us and the house. Brenda crawled up to the bush and pulled back the limbs. I crawled behind her. Brenda whispered, "There he is."

I looked through the limbs. There was a big man with a hat in his hands standing by The Old House. He was looking around for something. Probably us. He scratched his head and took a few steps toward us. He was looking up the hill where we were. We got down flat on the ground and were very quiet. I could hear my heart going. Brenda raised her head a little and said, "Oh, no! He's found the note. He's putting it in his pocket. He's looking around. He's going back down the hill! He must have a car down there."

Brenda whispered, "There he is."

We stood up then. We watched the man walk over the hill toward the road. We heard the car start up. It backed out onto the road. We ran down The Grassy Road to see where he went. The car moved slowly down the road and then stopped in front of my house. I said, "Oh, no!" the way Brenda does.

Brenda said, "We're dead meat."

I said, "I'm not old enough to be dead meat."

Even though it was cold, we sat down on the ground. We watched my house. The man had knocked on the door and then gone in.

I was breathing a lot and so was Brenda. I couldn't think of anything to say. Brenda threw her hands in the air and said it again. "We're dead meat."

She learned to say that when she was in school.

It was a long time before the man came out of my house. My mother and Brenda's mother were with him. He shook hands with them and went to his car.

When the big black car left, my mother shouted. "Bobby! Come down here. Bobby!"

And then Brenda's mother shouted. "Brenda! Come down here!" They shouted over and over.

Brenda and I went down the hill very slowly. I put my hands in my pockets and walked with my head down. Brenda stopped now and then to kick at the grass on The Grassy Road. We got to where they could hear us, and Brenda yelled, "What do you want?"

I looked at her like she was crazy. I said, "I know what they want."

She said, "We're dead meat."

We got down to the house, and my mother said, "Bobby, go to your room. Where are your mittens?"

I said, "I dropped them."

She said, "Never mind. I'll get them. You go to your room."

I said, "Yes, ma'am."

Brenda's mother said, "Brenda, go to your room."

Brenda said, "May I go to Bobby's room?"

Her mother said, "No, go to your room."

Brenda looked at me and bounced her shoulders up and down.

While I was sitting in my room, I started to get sick. I was sick to my stomach. I thought I would die. I knew it would make everybody sad when I died. It would make me sad, too. But I was sick to my stomach until I looked out the window and saw my mother and Brenda's mother coming back down the hill from The Old House. They were laughing and talking. It made me feel better to see them laughing. I hoped Brenda could see them, too.

When my mother came into the house, I was standing in the kitchen. She looked at me and said, "I thought I told you to go to your room." She was not laughing anymore.

I said, "Yes, ma'am." I went back to my room and lay down on my bed. I thought about how I was not old enough to go to school, not old enough to be brave, not old enough to worry about money and how I was dead meat. It was a sad day. It made me want to cry.

My father came home, and I could hear him talking to my mother in the kitchen. I couldn't hear what they were saying. It was a long time before my mother called me

It was a sad day.

into the living room. Brenda, her mother and father, and my mother and father were all there. They made Brenda and me sit on the sofa. They took turns talking to us about us. They said that the big man with the hat used to live in The Old House when he was a little boy. They said he went to school for a long time and got to be a doctor. They said he came home every year to see The Old House where his mother used to live until she died. They said he came home this year to tell The Old House goodbye. It was going to be torn down soon, they said. It was a long story and kind of sad, my mother said.

Then they started talking about how you can't go into other people's houses, even if they are empty and even if all you want to do is make a Christmas tree for Jesus. Brenda's father said that twice.

I saw a bug on the floor. I put my foot out to stop it going one way, and it started going the other. I put my other foot out to stop it from going that way. My mother said, "Bobby, stop that and pay attention."

I said, "Yes, ma'am."

Brenda's father said that since it was Christmas, they were not going to punish us.

I looked at Brenda for a second. Brenda looked at me. We didn't say anything.

Brenda's father said that if we ever did anything like that again, we would be punished. He had a list of things we wouldn't be able to do. Like watch TV, play with our toys, play together, and a lot of things we liked to do all the time. Brenda's mother said did we understand. Brenda said, "Yes, ma'am."

Then Brenda's father said that the big man with the hat had liked our tree a lot. The man had said so. He said it was easier for him to tell The Old House goodbye now because the tree was living there and being loved.

Christmas was pretty good after that. I got a red truck and a pair of gloves. Brenda got a record player of her own.

And one more thing. On Christmas morning when I came to look under the tree, there was a little package to Brenda and me. It was from the big man in the hat who used to live in The Old House. Inside the package was the card Brenda had made. It was the one that said, "We love you, Jesus" and was signed by Brenda and me. There was another card, too. It was from the man. It said, "Dear Bobby and Brenda, I'm not Jesus, but

. . . there was a little package to Brenda and me.

I know Him, and I think He would want me to thank you for His tree." The little package made me feel good, and Brenda, too.

After Christmas some men came and tore down The Old House and hauled it away. They were real careful. They said the big man had paid them extra to not hurt Jesus' Christmas tree.

Brenda and I were glad. We can hardly wait 'til next year. Brenda's got these shiny red buttons her grandmother gave her from an old dress, and I've already saved up seven new pop tabs.

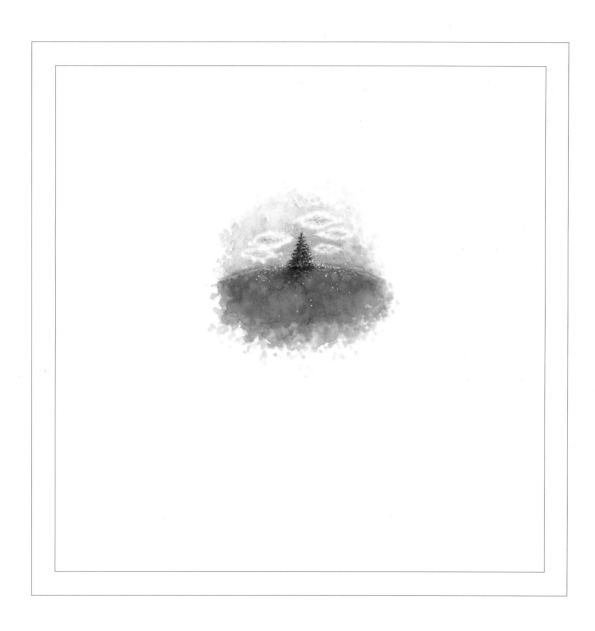

Mister Tom T. Hall was born in Olive Hill, Kentucky, and now makes his home in Franklin, Tennessee. A Grammy winner and a member of the Songwriters' Hall of Fame, he has won forty-six awards from the Broadcast Music Industry and has published a novel, a collection of short stories, an autobiography, and two songwriting handbooks.

Illustrator Laura L. Seeley, a native of Andover, Massachusetts, now lives in Atlanta, Georgia. She holds a Bachelor of Fine Arts degree from the Rochester Institute of Technology. Seeley has written and illustrated **THE BOOK OF SHADOWBOXES: A Story of the ABC's**, which will be published by Peachtree Publishers.